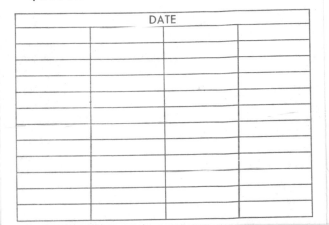

RAINY DAY

Stories and Poems

RAINY DAY

Stories and Poems

Edited by Caroline Feller Bauer

Illustrated by Michele Chessare

HarperCollins*Publishers*

Rainy Day: Stories and Poems
Text copyright © 1986 by Caroline Feller Bauer
Illustrations copyright © 1986 by Michele Chessare
All rights reserved. No part of this book may be
used or reproduced in any manner whatsoever without
written permission except in the case of brief quotations
embodied in critical articles and reviews. Printed in
the United States of America. For information address
HarperCollins Children's Books, a division of
HarperCollins Publishers, 10 East 53rd Street,
New York, NY 10022.

Library of Congress Cataloging-in-Publication Data
Main entry under title:
Rainy day.

Summary: A collection of stories and poems about rain
by a variety of authors.
1. Rain and rainfall—Literary collections. 2. Children's literature. [1. Rain and rainfall—Literary
collections. 2. Literature—Collections] I. Bauer,
Caroline Feller. II. Chessare, Michele, ill.
PZ5.R14 1986   808.8'036   85-45170
ISBN 0-397-32104-X
ISBN 0-397-32105-8 (lib. bdg.)

Designed by Constance Fogler
4 5 6 7 8 9 10

ACKNOWLEDGEMENTS

Every effort has been made to trace ownership of all copyright material and to secure the necessary permissions to reprint these selections. In the event of any question arising as to the use of any material, the editor and the publisher, while expressing regret for any inadvertent error, will be happy to make the necessary correction in future printings. Thanks are due to the following for permission to reprint the copyrighted materials listed below:

The American Museum of Natural History, for the "Traditional Crow Indian Poem" from The American Museum of Natural History, *Anthropological Papers*, 1922, Vol. 25 / Atheneum Publishers, Inc., for "Cloudy With a Chance of Meatballs" by Judi Barrett. Text copyright © 1978 Judi Barrett; "Outside" from *I Feel the Same Way*. Copyright © 1967. Lilian Moore. / Bell & Hyman, Publishers, for "Rainy Nights" by Irene Thompson from *Weathers and Seasons* compiled by Dennis Saunders and Terry Williams. / Borsky & Miller, for "The Jolly Tailor" from the *Jolly Tailor* published by David McKay Company, Inc. / Charles Bowen, for "The Rain It Raineth" from William Cole's *Oh. Such Foolishness*. Curtis Brown, Ltd., for "The Clock." Copyright © 1979 by Freya Littledale; "Instant Storm." Copyright © 1975 by X.J. Kennedy. / Dodd, Mead & Company, Inc. for "London Rain" from *Star in a Well* by Nancy Byrd Turner. Copyright © 1935 by Dodd, Mead & Co., Inc. Copyright renewed 1962 by Nancy Byrd Turner. / Doubleday & Company, Inc., for "I Know an Owl" by Edward Anthony from *Oddity Land* by Edward Anthony. Copyright © 1957 by Edward Anthony. / E.P. Dutton, for "This Year" and "Summer Storm" from *Wind, Sand and Sky* by Rebecca Caudill. Copyright © 1976 by Rebecca Caudill. / John Holmes, for "Rhyme of Rain" from *On City Streets*. / Holt, Rinehart & Winston publishers, for "I Stare" from *Come Along* by Rebecca Caudill. Copyright © by Rebecca Caudill. / Houghton Mifflin Company, for "Ka-Trum" from *Plink, Plink, Plink* by Byrd Baylor. Copyright © 1971 by Byrd Baylor. / Alfred A. Knopf, for "April Rain Song" from *The Dream Keeper and Other Poems* by Langston Hughes. Copyright © 1932 and renewed 1960 by Langston Hughes. / Karla Kuskin, for "When I Went Out" from *Dogs and Dragons, Trees and Dreams: A Collection of Poems* by Karla Kuskin. Copyright © 1958 by Karla Kuskin. / Brian Lee, for "Rain" from *Late Home* by Brian Lee. Copyright © 1976 by Brian Lee. / J.B. Lippincott, for "Rain Sizes" from *The Reason for the Pelican* by John Ciardi. Copyright © 1959 by John Ciardi. Copyright © 1959 by The Curtis Brown Publishing Company. / Dell J. McCormick, for "When the Rain Comes Up From China" from *Tall Timber Tales* by Dell J. McCormick. The Caxton Printers, Ltd., Caldwell, Idaho. / Eve Merriam, for "Summer Rain" from *There is No Rhyme for Silver* by Eve Merriam. Published by Atheneum Publishers. Copyright © 1962 by Eve Merriam; "Weather" from *Catch a Little Rhyme* by Eve Merriam. Published by Atheneum Publishers. Copyright © 1966 Eve Merriam. / New Directions Publishing Corporation, for "The Red Wheelbarrow" from *Collected Earlier Poems* by William Carlos Williams. Copyright © 1938 by New Directions Publishing Corporation. / Marian Reiner, for "Rain-Walking" from *A Crazy Flight and Other Poems* by Myra Cohn Livingston. Copyright © 1969 by Myra Cohn Livingston. / Libby Stopple, for "Papa Says". Copyright © 1975 by Libby Stopple. / Chisachi Suefiro, for "I Like Summer Rain" by Chisachi Svehiro from *My Very Own Seasons*.

TO DON BRODIE

"The rain in Spain falls mainly in Oregon"

Contents

x

Rain. Plants love it. See them stand tall after a good downpour. City rain. It washes a city and makes it look new and clean again. The sounds of rain. They can be dancing and rhythmic or monotonous and sad.

You may not always feel the same way when it starts to rain. If you get caught in a storm in your best clothes, you may feel like a bedraggled water rat. But if you walk in the rain in a new yellow slicker and rubber boots, splashing through puddles can be an exhilarating experience. Rain can be annoying if you're planning a picnic. But if you're planting a garden, rain can be more welcome than a bright, sunny day.

Authors and poets think about rain just as you do when you look out the window. Depending on their mood they see rain as exciting and fascinating or annoying and unpleasant. There are many kinds of rain, and there are many different kinds of stories and poems about rain.

So find a comfortable chair, put up your umbrella, and READ ABOUT RAIN.

RAINY DAY

Stories and Poems

Cloudy with a Chance of Meatballs

JUDI BARRETT

If you move to a town called Chewandswallow don't be
surprised if suddenly meatballs start falling from the sky.
Because in this town it doesn't rain rain, it rains food.

We were all sitting around the big kitchen table. It was Saturday morning. Pancake morning. Mom was squeezing oranges for juice. Henry and I were betting on how many pancakes we each could eat. And Grandpa was doing the flipping.

Seconds later, something flew through the air headed toward the kitchen ceiling...and landed right on Henry.

After we realized that the flying object was only a pancake, we all laughed, even Grandpa. Breakfast continued quite uneventfully. All the other pancakes landed in the pan. And all of them were eaten, even the one that landed on Henry.

That night, touched off by the pancake incident at

3

breakfast, Grandpa told us the best tall-tale bedtime story he'd ever told.

"Across an ocean, over lots of huge bumpy mountains, across three hot deserts, and one smaller ocean...there lay the tiny town of Chewandswallow.

In most ways, it was very much like any other tiny town. It had a Main Street lined with stores, houses with trees and gardens around them, a schoolhouse, about three hundred people, and some assorted cats and dogs.

But there were no food stores in the town of Chewandswallow. They didn't need any. The sky supplied all the food they could possibly want.

The only thing that was really different about Chewandswallow was its weather. It came three times a day, at breakfast, lunch, and dinner. Everything that everyone ate came from the sky.

Whatever the weather served, that was what they ate.

But it never rained rain. It never snowed snow. And it never blew just wind. It rained things like soup and juice. It snowed mashed potatoes and green peas. And sometimes the wind blew in storms of hamburgers.

The people could watch the weather report on tele-

4

vision in the morning and they would even hear a prediction for the next day's food.

When the townspeople went outside, they carried their plates, cups, glasses, forks, spoons, knives and napkins with them. That way they would always be prepared for any kind of weather.

If there were leftovers, and there usually were, the people took them home and put them in their refrigerators in case they got hungry between meals.

The menu varied.

By the time they woke up in the morning, breakfast was coming down.

After a brief shower of orange juice, low clouds of sunny-side-up eggs moved in followed by pieces of toast. Butter and jelly sprinkled down for the toast. And most of the time it rained milk afterwards.

For lunch one day, frankfurters, already in their rolls, blew in from the northwest at about five miles an hour.

There were mustard clouds nearby. Then the wind shifted to the east and brought in baked beans.

A drizzle of soda finished off the meal.

Dinner one night consisted of lamb chops, becoming heavy at times, with occasional ketchup. Periods of peas

and baked potatoes were followed by gradual clearing, with a wonderful Jell-O setting in the west.

The Sanitation Department of Chewandswallow had a rather unusual job for a sanitation department. It had to remove the food that fell on the houses and sidewalks and lawns. The workers cleaned things up after every meal and fed all the dogs and cats. Then they emptied some of it into the surrounding oceans for the fish and turtles and whales to eat. The rest of the food was put back into the earth so that the soil would be richer for the people's flower gardens.

Life for the townspeople was delicious until the weather took a turn for the worse.

One day there was nothing but Gorgonzola cheese all day long.

The next day there was only broccoli, all overcooked.

And the next day there were brussel sprouts and peanut butter with mayonnaise.

Another day there was a pea soup fog. No one could see where they were going and they could barely find the rest of the meal that got stuck in the fog.

The food was getting larger and larger, and so were the portions. The people were getting frightened. Violent storms blew up frequently. Awful things were happening.

7

One Tuesday there was a hurricane of bread and rolls all day long and into the night. There were soft rolls and hard rolls, some with seeds and some without. There was white bread and rye and whole wheat toast. Most of it was larger than they had ever seen bread and rolls before. It was a terrible day. Everyone had to stay indoors. Roofs were damaged, and the Sanitation Department was beside itself. The mess took the workers four days to clean up, and the sea was full of floating rolls.

To help out, the people piled up as much bread as they could in their backyards. The birds picked at it a bit, but it just stayed there and got staler and staler.

There was a storm of pancakes one morning and a downpour of maple syrup that nearly flooded the town. A huge pancake covered the school. No one could get it off because of its weight, so they had to close the school.

Lunch one day brought fifteen-inch drifts of cream cheese and jelly sandwiches. Everyone ate themselves sick and the day ended with a stomachache.

There was an awful salt and pepper wind accompanied by an even worse tomato tornado. People were sneezing themselves silly and running to avoid the tomatoes. The town was a mess. There were seeds and pulp everywhere.

The Sanitation Department gave up. The job was too big.

Everyone feared for their lives. They couldn't go outside most of the time. Many houses had been badly damaged by giant meatballs; stores were boarded up and there was no more school for the children.

So a decision was made to abandon the town of Chewandswallow.

It was a matter of survival.

The people glued together the giant pieces of stale bread sandwich-style with peanut butter... took the absolute necessities with them, and set sail on their rafts for a new land.

After being afloat for a week, they finally reached a small coastal town, which welcomed them. The bread had held up surprisingly well, well enough for them to build temporary houses for themselves out of it.

The children began school again, and the adults all tried to find places for themselves in the new land. The biggest change they had to make was getting used to buying food at a supermarket. They found it odd that the food was kept on shelves, packaged in boxes, cans and bottles. Meat that had to be cooked was kept in large refrigerators.

Nothing came down from the sky except rain and snow. The clouds above their heads were not made of fried eggs. No one ever got hit by a hamburger again.

And nobody dared to go back to Chewandswallow to find out what had happened to it. They were too afraid."

Henry and I were awake until the very end of Grandpa's story. I remember his good-night kiss.

The next morning we woke up to see snow falling outside our window.

We ran downstairs for breakfast and ate it a little faster than usual so we could go sledding with Grandpa.

It's funny, but even as we were sliding down the hill we thought we saw a giant pat of butter at the top, and we could almost smell mashed potatoes.

Rain-Walking

MYRA COHN LIVINGSTON

Walk in the
raining
puddles of mud
puddlejump
over a pool
walk in the
raining the raining
of mud
the puddles of raining to
school
slickers wet yellow
red brick boots
plop
in the
puddlejumps
slop
walk in the
raining
of black mirror streets

walk in the
raining
won't
stop

The Clock

FREYA LITTLEDALE

The clock
stops
on rainy
Sundays.

Outside

LILIAN MOORE

I
am inside
looking outside
at the pelting
rain—
where
the outside world
is melting
upon my
window
pane.

Rain

BRIAN LEE

The lights are all on, though it's just past midday,
There are no more indoor games we can play,
No one can think of anything to say,
It rained all yesterday, it's raining today,
It's grey outside, inside me it's grey.

I stare out of the window, fist under my chin,
The gutter leaks drips on the lid of the dustbin,
When they say "Cheer up!," I manage a grin,
I draw a fish on the glass with a sail-sized fin,
It's sodden outside, and it's damp within.

Matches, bubbles and papers pour into the drains,
Clouds smother the sad laments from the trains,
Grandad says it brings on his rheumatic pains,
The moisture's got right inside of my brains,
It's raining outside, inside me it rains.

16

I Stare

REBECCA CAUDILL

I stare at the rain,
　And rain, like our old gray cat,
Stares coldly at mc.

London Rain

NANCY BYRD TURNER

When it rained in Devon,
Salt was on my lips;
I leaned against a gray wharf
And dreamed of old ships.

When it rained in Yorkshire,
I tarried indoors
And heard the weather calling
Up and down the moors.

But when it rained in London,
I couldn't stay still;
My feet, before I told them,
Had run to Pippin Hill.

Before I even knew it,
As wet as sops, my feet
Were splashing Dark Horse Alley
And Pickled Herring Street.

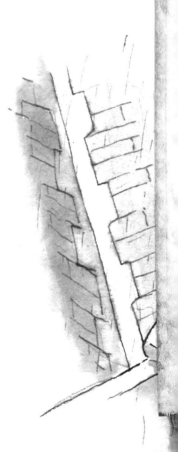

Through Pudding Court I paddled,
I waded Honey Lane—
The rain that falls on London
Is not like other rain.

Wet days are wild in Cornwall,
In Kent they're sweet and slow,
But when it rains in London,
Ah, when it rains in London,
You're drenched with long ago.

They say:

It will rain if an ant covers the hole of its anthill.

They say:

It will rain soon if cows are lying down in the pasture.

They say:

When the chairs squeak,
It's about rain they speak.

They say:

If the rooster crows at night
He's trying to say rain's in sight.

The Jolly Tailor

LUCIA MERECKA BORSKI
[*Lucia Merecka Szczepanowicz*]
AND KATE B. MILLER

*This is a folktale from Poland. In a town called Pacanów it
has been raining for an entire week. Yet all around the town it
is sunny and clear. How can this be? It's a lucky thing for these
townspeople that Nitechka the Tailor arrives with his needle
and thread. He will certainly solve their problem.*

Once upon a time, in the town of Taidaraida, there lived a
merry little Tailor, Mr. Joseph Nitechka. He was a very thin
man and had a small beard.

All tailors are thin, reminding one of a needle and
thread, but Mr. Nitechka was the thinnest of all, for he
could pass through the eye of his own needle. He was so
thin that he could eat nothing but noodles, for they were
the only thing which could pass down his throat. But for all
this, he was a very happy man, and a handsome one, too.

Now Mr. Nitechka would have lived very happily in
Taidaraida had it not been for a Gypsy. She happened to be
in the town when she cut her foot. In her trouble she went to

the Tailor, who darned the skin so carefully and so neatly that not a scar could be seen. The Gypsy was so grateful that she read Nitechka's future from his hand:

"If you leave this town on a Sunday and walk always Westward, you will reach a place where you will be chosen King!"

Nitechka laughed at this. But that very night he dreamt that he indeed became a King, and that from great prosperity he grew so fat that he looked like an immense barrel. Upon waking he thought:

"Maybe it is true? Who knows? Get up, Mr. Nitechka, and go West."

He took a bundle with a hundred needles and a thousand miles of thread, a thimble, an iron, and a pair of very big scissors, and started out to find the West.

But he had not gone far when a gust of wind blew across a field—not a very strong gust—but, because Mr. Nitechka was so exceedingly thin, just strong enough to carry him off.

The Tailor flew through the air, laughing heartily at such a ride. Soon, however, the wind became tired and let him down to earth. He was much bewildered and did not come to his senses until someone shouted:

"What is this?"

Mr. Nitechka looked around and saw that he was in a wheat field and that the wind had thrown him right into the arms of a Scarecrow. The Scarecrow was very elegant in a blue jacket and a broken stove-pipe hat, and his trousers were only a little bit torn. He had two sticks for feet and also sticks for hands.

Nitechka took off his little cap, bowed very low, saying in his thin voice:

"My regards to the honorable Sir. I beg your pardon if I stepped on your foot. I am Mr. Nitechka, the Tailor."

"I am very much pleased to meet such a charming man," answered the Scarecrow. "I am Count Scarecrow and my coat of arms is Four Sticks. I watch the sparrows here so that they will not steal wheat, but I give little heed to them. I am uncommonly courageous and would like to fight only with lions and tigers, but this year they very seldom come to eat the wheat. Where are you going, Mr. Nitechka?"

Nitechka bowed again and hopped three times as he was very polite and he knew that well-bred men thus greeted each other.

"Where do I go, Mr. Count? I am going Westward to a place where I will become King."

"Is it possible?"

"Of course! I was born to be a King. And perhaps you, Mr. Count, would like to go with me; it will be merrier."

"All right," answered the Scarecrow. "I am already weary of being here. But please, Mr. Nitechka, mend my clothes a bit, because I might like to marry someone on the way; and so I should be neat and handsome."

"With great pleasure!" said Mr. Nitechka, and in an hour the Scarecrow had a beautiful suit and a hat almost like new. The sparrows in the field laughed at him a little, but he paid no attention to them as he walked with great dignity with Mr. Nitechka.

On the way the two became great friends. They generally slept in a wheat field, the Tailor tying himself to the Scarecrow with a piece of thread so that the wind could not carry him off again.

When after seven days of adventures they reached the town of Pacanów, they were greatly astonished. All around the town it was sunshiny and pleasant; but over Pacanów the rain poured from the sky as from a bucket.

"I won't go in there," said the Scarecrow, "because my hat will get wet."

"And even I would not wish to become King of such a wet kingdom," said the Tailor.

Just then the townspeople spied them and rushed toward them, led by the Burgomaster riding on a shod goat.

"Dear Sirs," they said, "maybe you can help us."

"And what has happened to you?" asked Nitechka.

"Deluge and destruction threaten us. Our King died a week ago, and since that time a terrible rain has come down upon our gorgeous town. We can't even make fires in our houses, because so much water runs through the chimneys. We will perish, honorable Sirs!"

"It is too bad," said Nitechka very wisely.

"Oh, very bad! And we are most sorry for the late King's daughter, as the poor thing can't stop crying and this causes even more water."

"That makes it still worse," replied Nitechka, still more wisely.

"Help us, help us!" continued the Burgomaster. "Do you know the immeasurable reward the Princess promised to the one who stops the rain? She promised to marry him and then he will become King."

"Truly?" cried Nitechka. "Count Scarecrow, let's go to the town. We ought to try to help them."

28

They were led through the terrible rain to the Princess, who upon seeing Nitechka cried out:

"Oh, what a handsome youth!"

He hopped three times and said:

"Is it true, Princess, that you will marry the one who stops the rain?"

"I vowed I would."

"And if I do it?"

"I will keep my promise."

"And I shall become a King?"

"You will, O beautiful youth."

"Very well," answered the Tailor. "I am going to stop the rain."

So saying he nodded to Count Scarecrow and they left the Princess.

The whole population, full of hope, gathered around them. Nitechka and the Scarecrow stood under an umbrella and whispered to each other:

"Listen, Scarecrow, what shall we do to make the rain stop falling?"

"We have to bring back pleasant weather."

"But how?"

"Ha! Let's think!"

But for three days they thought and the rain fell and fell and fell. Suddenly Nitechka gave a cry of joy like a goat's bleating.

"I know where the rain comes from!"

"Where from?"

"From the sky!"

"Eh!" grumbled the Scarecrow. "I know that too. Surely it doesn't fall from the bottom to the top, but the other way around."

"Yes," said Nitechka, "but why does it fall over the town only, and not elsewhere?"

"Because elsewhere is nice weather."

"You're stupid, Mr. Count," said the Tailor. "But tell me, how long has it rained?"

"They say since the King died."

"So you see! Now I know everything! The King was so great and mighty that when he died and went to Heaven he made a huge hole in the sky."

"Oh, oh, true!"

"Through the hole the rain poured and it will pour until the end of the world if the hole isn't sewed up!"

Count Scarecrow looked at him in amazement.

"In all my life I have never seen such a wise Tailor," said he.

They rejoiced greatly, went to the Burgomaster, and ordered him to tell the townspeople that Mr. Joseph Nitechka, a citizen of the town of Taidaraida, promised to stop the rain.

"Long live Mr. Nitechka! Long may he live!" shouted the whole town.

Then Nitechka ordered them to bring all the ladders in the town, tie them together, and lean them against the sky. He took a hundred needles and, threading one, went up the ladders. Count Scarecrow stayed at the bottom and un-

wound the spool on which there was a hundred miles of thread.

When Nitechka got to the very top he saw that there was a huge hole in the sky, a hole as big as the town. A torn piece of the sky hung down, and through this hole the water poured.

So he went to work and sewed and sewed for two days. His fingers grew stiff and he became very tired but he did not stop. When he had finished sewing he pressed out the sky with the iron and then, exhausted, went down the ladders.

Once more the sun shone over Pacanów. Count Scarecrow almost went mad with joy, as did all the other inhabitants of the town. The Princess wiped her eyes that were almost cried out and, throwing herself on Nitechka's neck, kissed him affectionately.

Nitechka was very happy. He looked around, and there were the Burgomaster and Councilmen bringing him a golden scepter and a gorgeous crown and shouting:

"Long live King Nitechka! Long live he! Long live he! And let him be the Princess' husband and let him reign happily!"

So the merry little Tailor reigned happily for a long time, and the rain never fell in his Kingdom. In his good fortune Nitechka did not forget his old friend, Count Scarecrow, but he appointed him the Great Warden of the Kingdom to drive away the sparrows from the royal head.

33

April Rain Song

LANGSTON HUGHES

Let the rain kiss you.
Let the rain beat upon your head with silver liquid drops.
Let the rain sing you a lullaby.

The rain makes still pools on the sidewalk.
The rain makes running pools in the gutter.
The rain plays a little sleep-song on our roof at night—

And I love the rain.

Papa Says

LIBBY STOPPLE

Papa
Says rain
Makes things grow.

I stood out in the rain
All morning
With my toes in the mud,
But Granma says I really
Didn't get any Bigger.
It's just that my pants
Shrunk.

Rain Sizes

JOHN CIARDI

Rain comes in various sizes.
Some rain is as small as a mist.
It tickles your face with surprises,
And tingles as if you'd been kissed.

Some rain is the size of a sprinkle
And doesn't put out all the sun.
You can see the drops sparkle and twinkle,
And a rainbow comes out when it's done.

Some rain is as big as a nickel
And comes with a crash and a hiss.
It comes down too heavy to tickle.
It's more like a splash than a kiss.

When it rains the right size and you're wrapped in
Your rainclothes, it's fun out of doors.
But run home before you get trapped in
The big rain that rattles and roars.

I Know an Owl

EDWARD ANTHONY

I know an owl
  Who uses a towel
To dry himself after it rains.
"I hate being wet," he explains.

KA-TRUM

BYRD BAYLOR

KA-TRUM
KA-TRUM
KA-TRUN

When buffalo run
They darken the sun.
They cover the sky
When they pass by.
Tall grasses lie flat
And wild birds cry
And dry earth trembles
When they pass by.
But
Indian hunters
Stay quiet as the grass,
Quiet as the shadows
Where buffalo pass
Until the *zing* of an arrow
The *whish* of a spear,

Tell you they must be
Somewhere
Near.
Near *here?*
But what sounds like hoofbeats
Is pounding rain—
Not buffalo moving across a plain.
Just
Rain
Rain
Rain.

I Like Summer Rain

CHISACHI SUEHIRO

I like summer rain
On a quiet afternoon
When the rain drops shine in the pond
Like tiny crowns

This Year

REBECCA CAUDILL

This year the sweet rains
   Spring-clean the earth and lay
     A flower-gemmed carpet.

41

The Rain It Raineth

CHARLES BOWEN

The rain it raineth on the just
    And also on the unjust fella;
But chiefly on the just, because
    The unjust steals the just's umbrella.

When I Went Out

KARLA KUSKIN

When I went out to see the sun
There wasn't sun or anyone
But there was only sand and sea
And lots of rain that fell on me
And where the rain and river met
The water got completely wet.

SUNSHINE ON A STICK

Bring a little sunshine into a rainy day.
You need:

 a quart of orange juice
 an ice cube tray
 toothpicks
 clear plastic wrap

Pour orange juice into ice cube tray. Stretch the plastic wrap tightly over tray. Punch one toothpick into each cube through the plastic wrap. Freeze.

Eat your ice pops on a rainy day when you would like a bit of sunshine in your life.

WATER CHIMES

Fill stem glasses with varying amounts of water. Line them up in a row on a counter. Strike each one in turn gently with a spoon and listen to the music.

. . .

Write a poem about **rain** and fit it into a drawing of a raindrop.

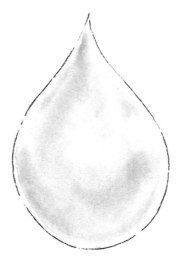

When the Rain Came Up from China

DELL J. McCORMICK

This Paul Bunyan story is a tall tale. What does that mean?
Imagine a group of loggers sitting around the bunkhouse after
a hard day of work in the forest. They start to swap stories.
Then they begin to exaggerate. The stories get wilder and
wilder—suddenly they're telling tall tales. In this one,
someone remembers the time the rain came up from China.

The year Paul Bunyan came west he had a big camp near the mouth of the Columbia River. It was probably the biggest logging camp the West Coast ever knew. The bunkhouses stretched for miles in all directions and each had five tiers of bunks, one above the other.

The dining room was a problem with so many men to feed. Ole built a giant soup kettle that covered five and a half acres and sent for a Mississippi stern-wheeler. It was quite a sight with the fire burning merrily under it and the old steamer paddling around mixing up vegetable soup for

dinner. One day a team of oxen fell in but it didn't worry Sourdough Sam any. He just changed the menu to "beef broth" that night and everybody seemed mighty pleased with the result.

The waiters wore roller skates, but the tables were so long they used to wear out two and three pair of skates just making the rounds with hot coffee. Tiny Tim the Chore Boy drove the salt and pepper wagon. He usually drove the length of the table and stayed all night at the far end, driving back to the kitchen in the morning for a fresh load. It took so much time getting all the men into the dining room some of them almost starved to death waiting their turn. Paul finally had to build lunch counters outside where the men waiting in line could get a light lunch in the meantime.

Paul expected a wet damp winter in the Douglas fir country, but month after month went by and never a sign of rain. He had all the bunkhouse roofs lined with thick tar paper to keep out the rain. The men were given rainproof slickers to put on over their mackinaws, and Babe the Blue Ox had a big tarpaulin for his own use. It was made from the canvas of Barnum and Bailey's main tent and fitted him fine except that it was a little short around the knees.

Just when they least expected it, however, it began to rain, and it was the strangest rain that anyone ever saw! Instead of raining down it rained up! The earth fairly spouted water. It filled the men's boots. It rained up their sleeves. It went up their pant legs in spite of everything they could do. It was impossible to escape! Naturally the rain coats and the tarpaulins and the tar roofs on the bunkhouses were useless, for the rain was coming up from below.

It seeped through the bunkhouse floors and flooded the cook shanty. Men crawled into the top bunks to escape and floated from one bunk to another on homemade rafts.

Hot Biscuit Slim and Sourdough Sam cooked the evening
meal floating around the kitchen on flour barrels. Cream
Puff Fatty sat in an empty tub and paddled back and forth
to the stove cooking apple pies.

Johnnie Inkslinger looked at the rain coming up from
the ground and cried in great surprise:

"It's raining from China!"

Up from China came the bubbling rain until the
whole forest was one vast swamp. Little fountains of water
sprang up everywhere. It rained in the men's faces when
they bent over to pick up a cant hook or peavey. It spurted

51

up their coatsleeves and ran down their backs inside their heavy mackinaws. A knothole in the bunkhouse floor started a geyser of water ten feet high. Paul decided to turn the bunkhouses upside down so the tar paper roofs would keep the water out. By that time the water was well up to his ankles, which meant that it would come up to the armpit of the average man.

Just as Paul had about decided to abandon the camp, the rain from China stopped as quickly as it began. The water seeped back into the moist earth, and by nightfall most of the water had disappeared except in pools here and there throughout the woods. Paul breathed a sigh of relief to find his feet on solid ground again, and the men built huge campfires to dry out their soaked clothing.

It was many years, however, before the lumberjacks in Paul's camp forgot their terrible experience with the rain that came from China. Even now when some camp orator starts to tell about a terrific rainstorm an old-timer will shake his head slowly and remark:

"Stranger, you don't even know what rain is unless you was with Paul Bunyan out in Oregon. You ain't never seen rain nor got wet unless you was working with Paul Bunyan out west the year the rain came up from China!"

Rhyme of Rain

JOHN HOLMES

"Fifty stories more to fall,
Nothing in our way at all,"
Said a raindrop to its mate,
Falling near the Empire State.
Said the second, "Here we go!
That's Fifth Avenue below."
Said the first one, "There's a hat.
Watch me land myself on that.
Forty stories isn't far—
Thirty-seven—here we are—
Twenty, sixteen, thirteen, ten—
"If we make this trip again,"
Said the second, "we must fall
Near a building twice as tall."
"What a time to think of that,"
Said the first, and missed the hat.

Summer Storm

REBECCA CAUDILL

The summer storm comes
   Bolting white lightning; it goes
    Muttering thunder.

55

Rainy Nights

IRENE THOMPSON

I like the town on rainy nights
    When everything is wet—
When all the town has magic lights
    And streets of shining jet!

When all the rain about the town
    Is like a looking-glass,
And all the lights are upside-down
    Below me as I pass.

In all the pools are velvet skies,
    And down the dazzling street
A fairy city gleams and lies
    In beauty at my feet.

When the Day Is Cloudy

TRADITIONAL CROW INDIAN POEM

When the day is cloudy,
The thunder makes a low rumble
And the rain patters against the lodge,
Then it's fine and nice to sleep,
    isn't it?

The Red Wheelbarrow

WILLIAM CARLOS WILLIAMS

so much depends
upon

a red wheel
barrow

glazed with rain
water

beside the white
chickens

Summer Rain

EVE MERRIAM

A shower, a sprinkle,
A tangle, a tinkle,
Greensilver runs the rain.

Like salt on your nose,
Like stars on your toes,
Tingles the tangy rain.

A tickle, a trickle,
A million-dot freckle
Speckles the spotted rain.

Like a cinnamon
Geranium
Smells the rainingest rain!

Instant Storm

X. J. KENNEDY

One day in Thrift-Rite Supermart
My jaw dropped wide with wonder,
For there, right next to frozen peas,
Sat frozen French-fried thunder,
Vanilla-flavored lightning bolts,
Fresh-frozen raindrop rattle—
So I bought the stuff and hauled it home
And grabbed my copper kettle.

I'd cook me a mess of homemade storm!
But when it started melting,
The thunder shook my kitchen sink,
The ice-cold rain kept pelting,
Eight lightning bolts bounced round the room
And snapped my pancake turners—
What a blooming shame!
        Then a rainbow came
And spanned my two front burners.

Weather

EVE MERRIAM

Dot a dot dot   dot a dot dot
Spotting the windowpane.
Spack a spack speck   flick a flack fleck
Freckling the windowpane.

A spatter a scatter   a wet cat a clatter
A splatter a rumble outside.
Umbrella umbrella umbrella umbrella
Bumbershoot barrel of rain.

Slosh a galosh   slosh a galosh
Slither and slather and glide
A puddle a jump a puddle a jump
A puddle a jump puddle splosh
A juddle a pump aluddle a dump a
Puddmuddle jump in and slide!

Raindrops are perfectly round, not teardrop shaped.

In Saudi Arabia people use water that has been stored for 10,000 years in underground streams under the desert floor.

A rainbow is seen
When the sun is behind you and it's raining in front of you.

It hasn't rained for over 400 years in the Atacama Desert in Chile.

It rains 350 days a year on the island of Maui in Hawaii.

Something to Read
. . .
Index

Something to Read

PICTURE BOOKS

All Wet! All Wet! by James Skofield. Illustrated by Diane Stanley.
Harper, 1984.
*A small boy experiences, along with the animals of the
meadow and forest, the sights, smells, and sounds of a rainy
summer day.*

Caught in the Rain by Beatriz Ferro. Illustrated by Michele
Sambin. Doubleday, 1980.
*The places you can go to be sheltered from the rain are
poetically described.*

Ernest and Celestine's Picnic by Gabrielle Vincent. Illustrated by
the author. Greenwillow, 1982.
A picnic in the rain can be fun.

It's Going to Rain! by Ada B. Litchfield. Illustrated by Ruth M.
Hartshorn. Atheneum, 1980.
*Rhymed text shows various Cape Cod characters announcing
an approaching storm.*

Noah's Ark by Peter Spier. Illustrated by the author. Doubleday,
1977.
And it rained for 40 days and 40 nights...

69

Rain by Robert Kalan. Illustrated by Donald Crews. Greenwillow, 1978.

Rain falls on the black road, the red car, and the orange flowers.

Rain by Peter Spier. Illustrated by the author. Doubleday, 1982.

A wordless picture book shows two children enjoying a rainstorm.

Rainy Day Together by Ellen Parsons. Illustrated by Lillian Hoban. Harper, 1971.

A little girl and her mommy enjoy a rainy day together.

Storm at the Jetty by Leonard Everett Fisher. Illustrated by author. Viking, 1981.

Levi watches a thunderstorm.

Taste the Raindrops by Anna Grossnickle Hines. Illustrated by author. Greenwillow, 1983.

"I want to go walking in the rain."

The Rain Cloud by Mary Rayner. Illustrated by author. Atheneum, 1980.

A rain cloud floats through a summer day making some people sad and some people happy.

Umbrella by Taro Yashima. Illustrated by author. Viking, 1958.

Momo receives an umbrella for her birthday, but it never seems to rain so she can use it.

Will It Rain? by Holly Keller. Illustrated by author. Greenwillow, 1984.

Animal friends wait for a storm.

"In Which Piglet Is Entirely Surrounded by Water" in *Winnie-the-Pooh* by A. A. Milne. Illustrated by Ernest H. Shepard. Dutton, 1974.

Piglet is stranded when "it rained, and it rained, and it rained...."

Rainy Rainy Saturday by Jack Prelutsky. Illustrated by Marilyn Hafner. Greenwillow, 1980.

Poems to read on a rainy Saturday.

"Singing in the Rain" in *New Neighbors for Nora* by Johanna Hurwitz. Illustrated by Susan Jeschke. Morrow, 1979.

Nora and Teddy take a shower in the rain.

The Cay by Theodore Taylor. Doubleday, 1969.

Phillip and Timothy prepare for a devastating tropical storm.

The Night the Water Came by Clive King. Crowell, 1982.

Apu survives a storm and tells his story into a tape recorder.

Unicorns in the Rain by Barbara Cohen. Atheneum, 1980.

In the near future, Nikki becomes involved with an odd family that is building a huge ark for the coming rainstorm.

Us and Uncle Fraud by Lois Lowry. Houghton, 1984.

Marcus and Louise are separated in the midst of a storm.

Water for the World by Franklyn M. Branley. Illustrated by True Kelley. Crowell, 1982.

Water is important to us. Where does it come from? How do we use it?

71

Index